Phonics Stories Advanced Long and Short Vowel Patterns

Laurie Hunter

Illustrated by Gabrielle Watson

Published by Laurie Hunter
Austin, TX

Books by Laurie Hunter
Cultivating Reading and Phonics Skills 1st Grade – 3rd Grade
Phonics Stories - Short Vowels - Level 1
Phonics Stories - Long Vowels - Level 2
Phonics Stories - The Other Vowel Sounds - Level 3
Phonics Stories - Advanced Long and Short Vowel Patterns - Level 4
Cultivating Respect and Cooperation in the Classroom and at Home

Library of Congress Publisher's Cataloging-in-Publication Data
Names: Hunter, Laurie, 1969- author. | Watson, Gabrielle, 1993- illustrator.
Title: Phonics stories, advanced long and short vowel patterns / Laurie Hunter ; Gabrielle Watson, illustrator.
Description: Austin, TX : Laurie Hunter, 2023. | Summary: Nine stories introduce advanced long and short vowel patterns followed by word study and SEL topics. | Audience: Grades 1-4.
Identifiers: LCCN 2022918921 (print) | ISBN 978-0-9974882-4-1 (paperback) | ISBN 979-8-9879902-1-6 (audiobook)
Subjects: LCSH: High interest-low vocabulary books. | Reading--Phonetic method--Study and teaching (Elementary) | CYAC: Reading--Phonetic method. | Vowels. | Reading (Elementary) | Learning disabilities. | BISAC: JUVENILE FICTION / Readers / Beginner | JUVENILE FICTION / Concepts / Words.
Classification: LCC PZ7.1.H86 Ph 2023 (print) | LCC PZ7.1.H86 (ebook) | DDC [E]--dc23.

Publisher: Laurie Hunter
Cover Design: Bojan/Pixelstudio
Cover and Interior Illustrations: Gabrielle Watson
Interior Design: Ramona Andrea Fagaras

Level 4: For intermediate beginner readers, all ages, all abilities
Guided Reading Level: I - K

THE FIELD TRIP

My niece is a happy baby.

My niece is a happy baby with curly hair.
She has curly hair and a pretty smile.

My niece and I went on a field trip to a bakery. At the bakery, we learned how to make cookies and candy.

After the field trip, my niece and I saw a funny movie.
We ate cookies and candy at the movie.
It was a fun day with my niece!

Instructors, you have the option to preview the Spelling Words from "The Field Trip" with students before they attempt reading the phonics story. More importantly, after students read each phonics story, ask them to practice spelling the words with **ie** and **y** below.

Long e ie	Long e y
niece	hap-py
field	ba-by
cook-**ie**	cur-ly
cook-**ies**	pret-ty
mov-**ie**	ba-ker-y
can-d**ies**	can-dy
	fun-ny

Instructors, below are Vocabulary Words that can be discussed with the student after reading my letter on the following page.

Vocabulary from my letter
aunt, uncle, niece, nephew
field trip
learn
coronavirus pandemic
conversations
connection
collaborate
habit

Dear Reader,

Not everyone is lucky enough to have a big family. But, we all have someone special in our lives. Who is special to you? Is there something you would like to do with that person?

It can be difficult to spend time with someone who lives far away. At the beginning of the coronavirus pandemic, I was not able to be with any of my family. So, I set up regular video calls with them, and it was fun to see their faces and hear their voices. We talked and sometimes we played games during our video calls! Other times we would eat during our call, so it felt like we were having dinner together.

During our video chats, someone in the family would ask questions like, "What is the most surprising thing that happened to you this week?" and "What is a problem for you right now and how are you trying to solve it?" Everyone took turns sharing. It was fun. We all ended up experiencing many blessings from that unique time together. Our connections with one another helped us get through our difficult times.

During the coronavirus pandemic, I also began writing letters to friends and family. Is there someone you'd like to call, write a letter to, or video call? How could you connect and experience something together, even though you're apart?

Collaborate is a fancy word for working with another on a special project. How could you collaborate with a friend, parent, cousin, aunt, uncle, or grandparent? What could you learn together?

What activities and interests would you like to enjoy and share with others? Painting, cooking, telling jokes, hiking, photography, dancing, journaling, carpentry, camping in your backyard, gardening, designing websites, planning online theme events, martial arts, or something else?

I promise, if you make a habit of spending time with family, they will help you get through hard times. So, make spending time with family a habit. Learn new things and take field trips together. Have fun!

Enjoy,
Laurie Hunter

JUST TRY

I saw the fly cry.
I saw the fly cry, and I asked why.

The fly said he did not know why he
was crying.
I said there must be a reason why.

The fly said the reason why is because he could not fly in the sky.

I asked him to dry his tears.
I asked him to dry his tears and try to fly again.

Oh my! He did fly in the sky.

He did not cry.
He thanked me for asking him to dry his
tears and try to fly again.

Instructors, you have the option to preview the Spelling Words from "Just Try" with students before they attempt reading the phonics story. More importantly, after students read each phonics story, ask them to practice spelling the words with **y** below.

Long i y
fly
cry
cry-ing
why
sky
dry
try
my

Instructors, below are Vocabulary Words that can be discussed with the student after reading my letter on the following page.

Vocabulary from my letter
whine
written expression
overwhelmed
essay
publish
overcome
inabilities
mistakes
encourage
faith

Dear Reader,

When you're crying or whining, find out why. Is it because there's something you need or something you want?

Instead of crying or complaining, ask yourself "What can I do?" And ask others to encourage you to get the things you need and want.

Do you know that I have dyslexia? Dyslexia is a difficulty with learning to read. I struggled with reading and spelling for a long time, and it affected my written expression. There were times when I felt overwhelmed by how much I had to read and write. When I was in school, I remember crying while I was writing an essay.

But just because reading, spelling, and writing started out difficult, does that mean it will always be that way? Definitely not! The girl (me) who couldn't read in first grade, ended up later in life teaching children and teens how to read. I even created my own reading program for instructors and parents to teach their children how to read. And that girl (me) who once cried because she couldn't write a one-page essay for school ended up publishing her first book that was 163 pages long!

How did I overcome my inabilities? I worked hard and learned what would make me a better reader, writer, and speller. I listened to teachers and people who encouraged me. And I didn't give up. I kept reading and writing and learning from my mistakes.

I'm still learning from my mistakes. We all are. We just have to keep trying.

What is hard for you? What could you learn? Who could you ask to encourage you to keep trying?

I have faith in you. I know you can do it! Do your best, keep trying, and never give up.

Love,
Laurie Hunter

13

THE BRAVE KNIGHT AND THE BRIGHT FAIR MAID

A knight saw a dragon.

The knight saw a dragon high in a cave.

The dragon breathed fire.

He breathed fire that could light up the darkest night!

A maid yelled, "Help!" from inside the cave.
The brave knight said, "Dragon, release her
or I shall fight you!"

The dragon said, "I am not frightened of you.
Try to fight me with all your might."
As the dragon breathed fire, he did not see
or hear the fair maid run down the hill!

The brave knight and the fair maid raced back to the castle.

The maid asked the knight, "Are you
all right?"

The knight said, "Well, I was frightened.
But it is important to fight for what is right.
Lucky for me, you were bright. You ran, so I
did not have to fight for what was right!"

Instructors, you have the option to preview the Spelling Words from "The Brave Knight" with students before they attempt reading the phonics story. More importantly, after students read each phonics story, ask them to practice spelling the words with **igh** below.

Long i
igh
kn**igh**t
l**igh**t
n**igh**t
h**igh**
f**igh**t
fr**igh**t
m**igh**t
r**igh**t
br**igh**t

Instructors, below are Vocabulary Words that can be discussed with the student after reading my letter on the following page.

Vocabulary from my letter	
knight	injustice
maid(en)	unfairness
take advantage	authentic conversations
overwhelmed	cope
disrespected	adversity
prevent	sarcastic

Dear Reader,

There are different types of fighting. What are some types you can think of? Classmates can fight with their fists, parents can yell angry words, countries can fight with weapons. Those are just a few examples.

In the story, the knight was willing to fight the dragon to save the maid's life. But the maid was smart and escaped while the dragon was distracted. Wasn't that better than having to fight?

Fighting doesn't seem to solve problems. Usually, fighting causes more problems. So, why do you think people do it?

There are so many reasons. Think back when you yelled angrily or fought with someone. Why do you think you did that?

Most often, we lash out in anger at someone because that person hurt us or someone we care about. Or that person took advantage of us or someone we love. When we feel overwhelmed, hurt, or disrespected, we can be weak and swing our words or fists at someone. What can we do to prevent getting to that point?

The answer is not easy, but we must try to look for ways to prevent ourselves from reaching that point. Could we learn how to use our words and actions to tell others when we've been hurt, disrespected, or treated unfairly? Could we learn better ways to fight injustice and unfairness? Could we learn how to develop our communication skills so we can have authentic conversations? Could we learn how to develop better skills that help us cope with adversity and frustration? Could we practice patience? Could we learn ways to prevent ourselves from reacting violently or sarcastically?

Yes, we can.

Love,

Laurie Hunter

THE TEEN BLOWFISH AND THE OLD GOLDFISH

The old goldfish asked the teen blowfish, "What do you want to be when you grow up?"

The teen said, "I don't know. When I grow up, I think I will go with the flow."

The old fish said, "If you go with the flow, that is like throwing away gold. I am a goldfish. I don't want you to throw away gold!"

The old fish said, "Dear young blowfish, how would you like your life to be when you are older?"

The teen blowfish said, "I want to be a better student."

"If you want to be a better student, then sow seeds that will make you grow.

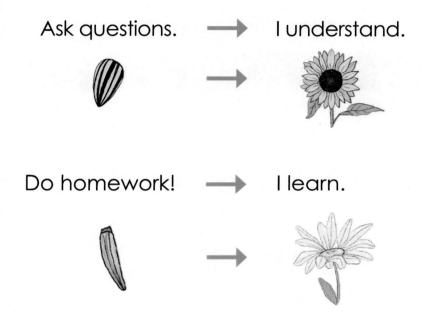

Ask questions. ⟶ I understand.

Do homework! ⟶ I learn.

Dear reader, how would you like your life to be when you are older?
What "seeds" can you sow?

Instructors, you have the option to preview the Spelling Words from "The Teen Blowfish and the Old Goldfish" with students before they attempt reading the phonics story. More importantly, after students read each phonics story, ask them to practice spelling the words with **ol** and **ow** below.

Long o ol	Long o ow
old	blow
gold	grow
told	know
	flow
	throw
	throw-ing
	sow

 Instructors, below are Vocabulary Words that can be discussed with the student after reading my letter on the following page.

Vocabulary from my letter
select
power
connected
controller
going with the flow
level up
making choices and decisions
taking action

Dear Reader,

The seeds in the story are an example of figurative language. When we speak figuratively, it is not meant to be taken literally. It would be nice for you to literally plants seeds in the earth. However, the seeds in the story are a metaphor that represent choices and decisions we make. When we decide what we'd like to happen in the future, we can make choices today (and every day) to get closer to reaching our goals. Dear reader, I want you to plant "seeds" that have the potential to "grow" something beautiful in your future.

If this is still confusing, here is another metaphor for you to consider. If you want to play Mario Kart, you have to select Mario Kart and not another game. You wouldn't select Minecraft. Right? For the same reason, if there is something you would like to happen in school or in life, you have to choose it. We select the life we want in the future by making decisions every day. That's how you "select the game" and play it! (This is another example of figurative language.)

Also consider this. When you play a video game, the power must be on and the controller must be connected, right? If the controller isn't connected with a wire or wirelessly, then you can't control where you go in the game. If your controller is not connected, you can't play to roam or level up. "Plug in the controller" of your life by making good decisions and taking actions to reach your goals. Good decisions and right actions will take you where you want to go in life. Truth!

How would you like to "level up" at school or home?

What decisions and choices could you make? How is this different from "going with the flow?"

Love,
Laurie Hunter

THE BABOON, HIS LOOSE TOOTH, AND THE KANGAROO

It was noon at the zoo and the baboon was moody.

He had a loose tooth and could not chew any food.

"Boohoo!" cried the moody baboon.

"My tooth hurts!"

The kangaroo said to the baboon, "I know just what to do!"
He said, "It will hurt, but I will pull out your loose tooth."

He reached into his pouch for his loose tooth tool.

With his handy tool, the kangaroo yanked out the baboon's loose tooth.

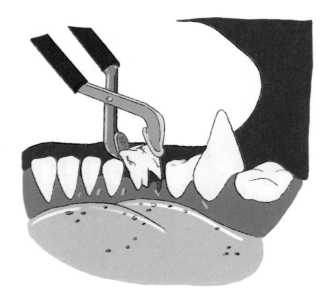

The baboon cried a few tears.

But soon, the hurt stopped and he was no longer gloomy.

The baboon thanked the kangaroo
because now he could chew his food!

Instructors, you have the option to preview the Spelling Words from "The Baboon, His Loose Tooth, and the Kangaroo" with students before they attempt reading the phonics story. More importantly, after students read each phonics story, ask them to practice spelling the words with **oo** and **ew** below.

Long u oo	Long u ew	Long u Says "oo" also
noon	chew	do
zoo	few	to
bab-oon		
mood-y		
loose		
tooth		
food		
boo-hoo		
kan-ga-roo		
tool		
soon		
gloom-y		

Instructors, below are Vocabulary Words that can be discussed with the student after reading my letter on the following page.

Vocabulary from my letter	
"pretty"	jealous
difficulties	struggles
tempted	moody
advantages	trust
problems	judge

Dear Reader,

Sometimes we think the "pretty" girl or the "popular" classmate has it so easy. We may think the "smartest" person in the class doesn't have to work as hard as everyone else. But is this really true? No!

You don't know what difficulties others have gone through. The truth is the "pretty" girl feels ugly just as often as everyone else. The "popular" guy has been bullied. The "smart" person feels "dumb" at times and makes mistakes also. So why do we judge others?

Sometimes we are tempted to think poorly of others when we are jealous of what advantages they have or problems they don't have. When we struggle with something difficult, we tend to think that everyone else has it so much easier. But they don't. Everyone struggles with different things on different days. We all experience pain and hurt feelings.

In the story, the baboon was moody because he had a loose tooth. When we're in pain, we should tell someone we trust, like he told the kangaroo. It's good to share our pain with others close to us. They can help.

And when others are moody and mean to us, it's best not to judge them, because they could be worrying or suffering. Maybe their pet died, or someone yelled at them that morning, or their parents fought the night before? We don't know. So, when a classmate, brother, sister, parent, teacher, or anyone is being mean, we should not be sad or get mad back. Instead, we could ask them, "Are you okay? What can I do to make it better?"

What if we all did this? How would it improve our family time, class time, and other times you can think of?

Take care,
Laurie Hunter

THE HAWK AND THE FAWN

The hawk was sitting in a tree.
The hawk in the tree saw a fawn on the lawn.

The fawn saw the hawk.
The fawn asked the hawk to play ball.

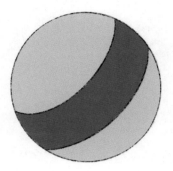

The hawk said, "I'd love to play ball. But, I can't because my short legs cannot kick a ball."

The fawn asked, "Would you like to draw?"

The hawk said, "I can't because my wings cannot hold a pencil to draw. Would you like to fly with me?"

The fawn said, "I can jump. But I cannot fly because I do not have wings. But these differences are not faults. We don't have to play ball, draw, or fly to have fun. We can talk!"

Instructors, you have the option to preview the Spelling Words from "The Hawk and the Fawn" with students before they attempt reading the phonics story. More importantly, after students read each phonics story, ask them to practice spelling the words with **aw, au,** and **al** below.

Short o aw sounds like octopus	Short o au sounds like octopus	Short o al sounds like octopus
hawk	be-cause	ball
saw	faults	talk
fawn		
lawn		
draw		

Instructors, below are Vocabulary Words that can be discussed with the student after reading my letter on the following page.

Vocabulary from my letter
judge
personal backgrounds
experiences
skills
abilities
communicate
discover

Dear Reader,

Before you judge someone else for not being able to do, think, speak, or look like you, ask yourself, "Should there only be hawks in this world? Should there only be fawns? Don't we need both hawks and fawns?"

People are all different. We all come from unique personal backgrounds and experiences. We each have various skills and abilities. Just because people are different, it doesn't mean one person is better than the other. Truth!

We must communicate and get to know each other. The more we talk to those who are "different," the more we will discover how alike we really are. But, we'll never know if we don't communicate with each other.

Love,
Laurie Hunter

MAMA PANDA

The mama panda went to a spa.
The mama panda went to the spa so she
could rest.

After she rested at the spa, she ate green pasta with a cup of water.

What a treat!

She said, "Ha ha! I like the spa and green pasta."
The mama panda felt rested.

Instructors, you have the option to preview the Spelling Words from "Mama Panda" with students before they attempt reading the phonics story. More importantly, after students read each phonics story, ask them to practice spelling the words with **a** (short u), **a** (short o), and **a** (short a) below.

Short u a sounds like umbrella	Short o a sounds like octopus	Short a a sounds like apple
pan-da	spa	pan-da
ma-ma	ma-ma	af-ter
pa-sta	pa-sta	at
what	wa-ter	and
a (the word "a" can be pronounced short u or long a)	ha ha !	

Instructors, below are Vocabulary Words that can be discussed with the student after reading my letter on the following page.

Vocabulary from my letter	
mama	maintain
expensive	repair
effort	deserve
energy	spa

Dear Reader,

Not everyone has a mama! But, everyone has someone who takes care of them. Who makes sure you have a place to sleep and food to eat? Who bought or gave you the clothes you are wearing?

Homes, cars, clothes, computers, doctor bills, phones, groceries, and eating out are very expensive. The person who takes care of you has to work very hard to make money to pay for things like these.

Also, it takes a lot of effort and energy to clean, maintain, and repair all the things that are in homes and cars. Who buys and makes the food you eat? Who cleans your clothes and the dishes? Who takes you to the doctor, dentist, and events? If you had to do all these things, would you want to work all day every day? Or would you like some time to rest?

The person(s) who takes care of you works very hard and deserves rest. Is there something nice you could do for someone who takes care of you?

Love,
Laurie Hunter

JEFF'S HOMEMADE BREAD

The bread was ready!
And, Jeff was ready to take the bread out
of the oven.
The bread was hot and heavy.

Jeff's hot and heavy bread made him sweat.
He felt the sweat drip from his head.

Jeff took a deep breath.
The hot and heavy bread made him sweat.
Jeff took a deep breath to smell the bread.
It smelled so good!

Jeff spread butter on his bread.
He took a bite.
The bread was so good, Jeff thought he
was dead and had gone to heaven!

I'm in heaven!

Instructors, you have the option to preview the Spelling Words from "Jeff's Homemade Bread" with students before they attempt reading the phonics story. More importantly, after students read each phonics story, ask them to practice spelling the words with **ea** and **e** below.

Short e ea sounds like elephant	Short e e sounds like elephant
bread	Jeff
read-y	ov-en
heav-y	felt
sweat	smell
head	smelled
breath	heav-en
spread	
dead	
heav-en	

Instructors, below are Vocabulary Words that can be discussed with the student after reading my letter on the following page.

Vocabulary from my letter	
whole wheat grain	cells
bread dough	nutritious
homemade food	work properly
packaged food	fresh ingredients
vitamins and minerals	recipe

45

Dear Reader,

My husband's name is Jeff, and his mother made homemade bread when he was younger. She taught him how to grind the dry whole wheat grain and how to make the bread dough rise. He makes bread often.

Does someone in your family make homemade food? Can you cook? Would you like to learn how to cook something?

Do you think homemade food is better for your body than packaged foods? Most packaged foods have less vitamins and minerals than homemade foods. Our bodies are made of cells that must have vitamins and minerals. If we don't eat nutritious foods, then over time our cells won't work properly.

When you make food from fresh ingredients, do you think it tastes better than packaged foods? It sure can!

I hope you learn recipes from your parent, grandparent, aunt, uncle, whoever! And, I hope you try to create some of your own special recipes too!

Love,

Laurie Hunter

LOVE

The son was young.
The young son misses his mother and dad.
He wonders about his mother and dad.

He does not have a brother or sister.

He was raised by his grandmother.

His grandmother loves him a ton.

She smothers him with love.

She is wonderful!

There is no other who loves him as much as his grandmother.

No one.

She loves me so much!

Instructors, you have the option to preview the Spelling Words from "Love" with students before they attempt reading the phonics story. More importantly, after students read each phonics story, ask them to practice spelling the words with **o** below.

Short u
o
sounds like umbrella
son
young
moth-er
grand-moth-er
broth-er
does
won-der
smoth-er
love
ton
oth-er
one (sounds like wun)

Instructors, below are Vocabulary Words that can be discussed with the student after reading my letter on the following page.

Vocabulary
emotions
positive
challenge
drugs
naturally
hobbies
interests

49

Dear Reader,

The boy in this story has a small family. It is just the two of them. He is blessed to have a grandmother who takes care of him and loves him. A lot of people have small families like the boy in the story. It can sometimes feel scary, lonely, or boring when others are not around. However, people in big families can feel these emotions too.

When we feel this way, it's important to turn to positive family members and friends, not to drugs, to help us feel better. People are most susceptible to take drugs when they are sad, mad, or scared. In life, we all feel these emotions. At times, we all may think that we are alone or that no one cares, but that is a lie! Don't believe it! There is ALWAYS someone who loves you. And that truth can help you stay strong during the hard times.

I challenge you to not take drugs. Drugs are not like you see in the movies and hear in songs. People on drugs can make bad choices that hurt others. And if you've already tried them, I challenge you to stop. It's never too late!

Even though I may not have met you, I care about you. If you are reading any of my books, then that makes you my student. And I am a teacher who loves all her students very much. I want you to be happy naturally, without drugs.

I challenge you to develop hobbies and interests that can help you deal with negative emotions. Writing your feelings down in a journal can help. Once you get the bad thoughts out on paper, then write three things or people you are grateful for. Most importantly, I encourage you to turn to positive family members and friends, and know that you are loved!

Love,

Laurie Hunter

GET TO KNOW THE AUTHOR AND ILLUSTRATOR

Laurie Hunter has been teaching children and teens of all abilities since 2005. She wrote the letters in this book to her students. She wants them, and you, to know that life can be joyful, even with all its traumas and challenges. Our good and bad experiences help us learn, make better decisions, and build character! Laurie wants you to know that you are not alone and that there is someone who loves you and needs you.

Gabrielle Watson has always had a passion for creating art, especially when it can help those around her learn something new! She wants to say thank you to the readers of this book and knows it can be challenging to tackle a new skill. Gabby wants you to know that no matter how large or small your goal may be, it all starts with a single step.

Made in the USA
Coppell, TX
12 September 2023

21493242R00031